LITTLE ROCK SECRET

Dr. Wyveta Kirk

A Christian Novella of Suspense and Romance

Wyveta Kirk/ SuccesSteps Publishing

www.wyvetakirk.com

Little Rock Secret/ Wyveta Kirk – 1st edition

Book Layout © 2014 BookDesignTemplates.com

ISBN 978-0-9915998-2-0
Ebook ISBN 978-0-9915998-3-7

Dedicated to the Special Men in My Life.

To my husband, Rod. Without his help I could not write. His engineering skills ensure accuracy of my formatting. His hours of proofreading and helping with home tasks provide me time to write.

To my older son, Todd, one of Las Vegas' best attorneys.

To my younger son, Trent, one of the smartest podiatrists in New Orleans.

To my grandson, Clay, who will make a great attorney upon graduation.

I cherish you guys, not for what you do, but for how you are and how you care about others.

I love you all.

CONTENTS

CHAPTER ONE

NO!

Emilie's face burned with fury. She grit her teeth. At this moment, she hated Connor. Maybe she hated him from day one. She degraded herself to help him, and he didn't appreciate anything. *"I hate him,"* she thought. *"I hate everything and everyone in my life. I can't take any more."* Emilie grabbed a long, thick carving knife from the drawer and turned to see Connor standing near the door ready to leave. Emilie lunged at him, screaming "I hate you!"

Connor turned and slapped her arm away so hard that Emilie fell backwards to the floor. She dropped the knife. It rolled beneath a table. Emilie lay lifeless. Connor stood staring down at her. He knew she hated him. He had known this for years. In fact, most days he felt the same about her. He knew no one who compared with her hypocrisy. He hated what a hypocrite she was. He never understood how she could be sweet and charming while they dated and turn so sour immediately after their wedding.

Several seconds passed as Connor stood staring at her. Then he asked, "Why aren't you moving?" He didn't expect a response but needed to say it aloud. Emilie hit her head on the sharp corner of a large box as she fell, but she remained unconscious much too long.

Perhaps he should call an ambulance. Maybe this was serious. Connor bent down and turned her head. There was no blood. He pressed on her neck to feel her pulse. No movement. He lifted her hand and felt her wrist. Nothing. He knelt to the floor and put his head on her chest. Emilie had no heart beat. "No! I think I killed her." Connor yelled with no one to hear.

Connor sat on the sofa. He needed to do something but what? He could not take his eyes off Emilie. He expected to see her move. An eyelid flicker or a finger wiggle. But there was no movement. Emilie was dead. He wished many times for an acceptable way to have her out of his life, but not this way. He never considered killing her. Divorce, but not killing her.

"But I didn't kill you," Connor said aloud as if Emilie could hear. "You tried to kill me. I only protected myself. But who would believe that? Who would believe me?" Connor needed to hear his own words to try to understand what happened and decide what to do next.

"She hated me, but she hated everyone. I know that. She would have won an award for being the friendliest, but she hated those with whom she seemed friendly," thought Connor. His mind flooded with memories of all their drives home after church how Emilie talked badly about everyone present. She thought the minister did a lousy job of presenting sermons. Every week she insisted she could plan a better lesson than he did. No matter what the minister said, his comments proved inadequate to Emilie.

Emilie worked at socializing as if she received pay for the number of people she hugged. If asked, others would say they liked Emilie. She asked everyone about their jobs and kids. When she saw them again, she remembered what they said in previous conversations and asked a related question. She sent expensive gifts to bridal and baby showers. When someone was ill, she ordered take-out meals sent to their home. She pretended to genuinely care about their lives. What others didn't know was, how after talking with them, she bragged that no one was as friendly as she was. Emilie needed to continually prove herself superior. Others loved Emilie, but she loved or respected no one.

Once on their drive home after worship Connor told Emilie the way she spoke negatively about others behind their backs was hypocritical and reminded her how God condemns hypocrisy. Emilie responded by slapping him, and almost caused him to have a wreck. Connor never mentioned it again. Telling her did no good. Emilie did not intend to change. *"But, hypocrisy can't be as wrong as murder,"* Connor now reasoned.

Connor sat on the sofa for what seemed like hours. Convinced that no one would believe he killed Emilie in self-defense, Connor knew he had to hide her body. *"The boat,"* thought Connor. *"She often goes out in the boat at night to paint the coastline in the moonlight. That's it. Yes, the boat."*

Connor wrapped Emilie's body in a large beach towel and lugged her to the boat. He steered the boat to the middle of the lake, splashed several cans of Emilie's paint thinner near the motors, and set the boat on fire. Once he knew the boat would blaze, Connor jumped in the dingy and paddled to the opposite side of the lake. He ran back to the cabin. Then keeping the lights off in his car until out of sight, he left for home.

Connor set his cruise control slightly below the speed limit. If stopped for speeding, his emotions would reveal something was wrong. He would be forced to lie if that happened, and he hated lying. He felt his strongest asset was truthfulness. In fact, his friends boasting his honesty helped secure his state senator seat. He couldn't let Emilie cause him to betray that reputation now.

She cheated him of enough in his life. She couldn't take his best character trait away too.

TWO YEARS LATER

Liddy, who is that brunette in the white dress standing by the terrace door?" asked Connor. "She blushes every time I catch her eye." Connor rarely attended Liddy's parties, but this one might prove worthwhile. He found the brunette attractive, and obviously she noticed him, at least enough to blush when they made eye contact.

"That's Abby, my cousin from Jonesboro," explained Liddy. "She's in town for a conference or seminar or something about her work. She phoned and asked if we could have dinner. I insisted that she come to my party and meet my friends. Want me to introduce you? She's single and, as far as I know, unattached."

"No, thanks," Connor said. "I think I will go introduce myself now that I know her name."

Connor moved to the door and stepped directly in front of Abby. "Hi," he said. "My name is Connor Cohen. I am a friend of Liddy. I rarely approach women I don't know, but I asked Liddy your name. Since she says you live in Jonesboro, I assume you don't know many people here. I thought we could visit and not feel so alone and out of place."

Abby blushed but liked the attention. "It's not much fun to linger in a room of strangers," she admitted. Like Connor, she wished for a way to escape.

"Well, I can't call them strangers," explained Connor. "I know their names, but I don't know any of them well enough to call them close friends either. How about us grabbing some punch, taking it outside, and telling each other our life stories? I'll get us something to drink and be right back." Connor turned and disappeared before Abby could respond.

When Connor left, Liddy moved quickly to update Abby. "Connor is single. His wife died a few years ago and to my knowledge he rarely dates. He lives in an expensive area of Little Rock and has a great business, a hand-me-down from his family. Besides, he's a state senator. He's attracted to you, so take time to meet him. You never know when such a contact may come in handy."

"But, what do I say to him? What do I know about a man with money and position? I'm not exactly a socialite." Before Liddy could argue, Connor returned. He handed Abby a drink and opened the door as Liddy sneaked Abby a goodbye wave.

In spite of multiple interruptions by people who wanted to speak to Connor, he managed to obtain Abby's phone number, home address, and the name of the hotel where she was staying. He convinced her to have dinner with him the following evening.

Abby agreed provided they met in the restaurant of the hotel where she stayed. She didn't know Little Rock well enough to venture farther, and she knew little about this man. At least not his character, values, or morals. That wasn't something she could learn talking briefly on a terrace. But, he was Liddy's friend, and she vouched for him.

Abby found Connor attractive. He filled the atmosphere with his charismatic personality as he talked freely about things he enjoyed. Abby realized that she smiled continually as she talked to him. She especially liked his humor.

Abby learned Connor had no children, rarely dated, read a lot, and a full-time housekeeper cooked his evening meals when he ate at home. He worked long hours and spent weekends working out at a gym. He spent most of his free time alone.

Connor proved a good listener and pressed Abby for information that she tended to keep to herself, especially about her family. "How lonely you must be with no relatives," said Connor. "I remember what a difficult time I experienced when each of my parents died." Connor's sensitivity touched Abby, as he continued pressing to learn more about her. "Are you and Liddy close?"

"No, Liddy never comes to Jonesboro to visit me. I phone when I plan to be in Little Rock, but that's usually once a year when I attend a seminar. We never talk by phone. So, no, I can't say we are close at all. We were closer as kids when our parents visited several times a year, but since our parents died, we haven't stayed in touch. Seems she and I live in two extremely different worlds."

Connor heard enough about Abby's history to know he wanted to know more. He loved how she blushed when he commented on her interests or paid her a compliment. She seemed genuine, far more than many of his friends. And she didn't visit with him because she wanted something from him, as many did who knew he was a senator.

Abby met Connor for dinner at her hotel, and by the time they finished eating, she agreed to meet for lunch the following day during her seminar break. Connor pressed Abby to remain in

Little Rock another night and promised to show her his view of the city. After much persuasion, she agreed, provided he understood that she wanted to leave in time to arrive home before dark. She hated driving alone that far.

Saturday, Connor arrived early to spend the day with Abby. He phoned her room from the lobby and told her he couldn't wait to see her. Upon her arrival, he helped check her luggage with the concierge.

Directing Abby to his car, he asked if there was someplace special she might like to see. Perhaps, someplace she never took the time to visit. Abby blushed and admitted, "I am ashamed to admit this, but I haven't been inside the Capitol since elementary school when our class came for a tour. Every year when I attend my conference, I think I will go, but I don't."

Connor turned the car to head to the Capitol. Along the way, he made a phone call and told Abby the man on the phone would meet them on the steps. "John knows the Capitol better than I do. He'll give us his twenty-five cent tour. I could use a good lesson on its history too. John knows the history of this city, who did what and when and why. He knows every nook and corner."

After the Capitol, Connor took Abby to Dizzy's, one of his favorite places for lunch. When she mentioned the last time she visited Hot Springs was when her parents took her as a child, Connor suggested they should go visit one of the bath houses. "It's a lovely drive, and I'll take a side trip and show you the beautiful lakes along the way."

After their bath house tour, Connor asked if Abby would like to try a bath, but Abby declined. She wanted to spend the time with him, not separated in some massage area alone with a masseuse. When she declined the bath, Connor insisted they should share a blackberry cobbler topped with a mountain-high scoop of ice cream. Across the street was Granny's Kitchen and they served a dish large enough for three people. Connor claimed it was the best cobbler in the state.

The waitress brought a huge serving with two spoons. Taking one bite, Abby said, "It melts in my mouth, Connor. This is wonderful. The crust is tender and perfect. The ice cream tastes like the homemade my mother used to make. It's rich and sweet. Thanks. I love it."

The last time Abby shared food from the same dish with anyone was when her father made her try his creation of caramelized strawberries topped with chocolate ice cream smothered in lemon sauce. It tasted horrible, but her dad's concoctions tended to become family jokes rather than treasured recipes. Abby liked eating from the same dish with Connor. Something about it made her feel close to him. It gave her a comfortable family feeling, a feeling she missed a lot.

Connor interrupted Abby's thoughts. "Ignore the large seeds in the blackberries. They lodge in every tooth. The waitress gives us a handful of toothpicks as we leave. We'll be like everyone else, picking our teeth as we wander down the street."

Abby smiled at Connor's comfort in breaking social etiquette. Her mother would definitely disapprove. She taught Abby never to pick her teeth in public.

On their drive back to Little Rock, Connor asked Abby several times to stay another night and spend Sunday with him, but she insisted she needed to go home. During her three years of teaching children at church, she had not missed one day and didn't want to miss one now. Connor said he understood but his facial expression betrayed his words.

"When can I see you again?" Connor asked. He paused, trying to let Abby control the next step.

"I will probably be here again next year for the same seminar. I attend every year."

Connor interrupted, "You know that isn't what I meant or intended. May I come to Jonesboro to see you? I can drive to Jonesboro in a couple of hours, and we can have dinner any night you are free. How about if I come Friday evening and stay over until late Sunday? I will go to church with you Sunday if that would be okay. You can show me your part of our state."

Abby agreed. She was free every night but Tuesday when she took an accounting course at Arkansas State.

Reluctantly, Connor returned Abby to her hotel and helped load her suitcase into her car. He turned to hug her. He wanted to kiss her, really kiss her, but he dated so little in the past few years he felt unsure if it would be appropriate. He didn't want to risk offending Abby. He enjoyed being with her too much to ruin things before they actually began. He kissed her on the check, pulled her close to hug her lightly for a few seconds, and opened her car door. He stood waving as she drove out of sight.

CHAPTER THREE

QUESTIONING HER FEELINGS

Thirteen red roses arrived for Abby at her workplace before 9:00 am Monday morning. The unsigned card read, 'Can't wait until the weekend.' Her workplace buzzed with gossip. Abby was not the type to display pictures or personal items in her work area, and roses on her desk were a first. However, she wasn't about to tell anyone who sent them.

Spending the weekend with a man she just met was a most unusual experience for Abby. Certainly, her reaction to Connor proved uncharacteristic. She shared little with others about her life away from work. She kept her personal life private, and her weekend with Connor would remain protected too. Besides, who sent the flowers was no one's business. If queried, she would say, "Just a friend." Time with Connor was another of her secrets.

However, the roses definitely impressed Abby. She read that when giving roses as a gift, you always give an odd number. She didn't know why it mattered, but it was obvious that Connor knew such social niceties.

Abby puzzled about her response to Connor. Rarely did she let anyone get this close, and certainly not this quickly. She shared things about her life with him that not even her best co-worker friend knew. If someone told her that some man she just met could persuade her to stay in town another night and spend the day with him, Abby would have insisted they were crazy. Her actions conflicted with everything she believed about herself. Her thoughts remained a tangle of questions, *"Why couldn't I tell Connor no? Was he that persuasive, or am I losing it? Am I so hungry for attention that I will do whatever he asks? No. No, that can't be me."* Her private thoughts filled with images of Connor during every free moment.

Abby questioned if she would feel more comfortable sharing more about her life with others if her parents had not been killed in a car wreck when she was a budding teenager. Her parents lived active social lives. They often visited with large groups of friends and took an enthusiastic role in Abby's activities. She didn't recall keeping things secret back then.

Before her parent's accident, Abby was outgoing. She held the lead role in her school play and served as president of two clubs, but after their sudden death, she became sullen and withdrawn.

The day her parents died, Abby was at home stringing colored paper and balloons for her 16th birthday party. Her parents slipped away to get her cake and party favorites. A police officer who was friends with her parents went to the home to tell her about their accident. A large truck overturned, hit their car, and pushed them into a deep ravine. Both died upon impact. Hearing the news, Abby collapsed and woke to find her best friend and minister from church with her. The officer phoned them before telling Abby. He knew she needed someone with her.

Abby's only living relatives at the time were Liddy's parents. She couldn't go live with them because Liddy's dad had cancer, and her mother suffered a stroke that left her partially paralyzed. She had no one. Abby's minister helped her to relocate to Paragould Children's Home, where her life changed beyond imagination.

At the Home, Abby lost all privacy. She shared a bedroom with two other girls, but the worst part was losing touch with her longtime friends. The Home was located several miles from Jonesboro, and few of her friends drove. The few who did were not allowed to drive out of town. Abby's parents left her a small amount of money, but it was held in a trust. She couldn't tap into the trust to buy a car until she turned 21. Gradually, she lost all contact with her Jonesboro friends and felt isolated at her new school.

Abby no longer participated in school events. She changed from being an open, chatty teenager who made friends easily to living in an empty, introverted shell. Regardless of how many students attempted to befriend Abby, she felt a continual sense of emptiness, a deep hungry void in her life. She never understood why she felt such feelings unless it reflected how deeply she missed her parents. Abby blamed their absence for the changes in her personality and convinced herself that she would still be outgoing and popular if her parents were alive. She often experienced thoughts about their accident being her fault. *"If I hadn't insisted on having a party, they wouldn't have been in the car that day."*

Since her parent's death, Abby feared telling others what she really thought about things. She worried what others might think about her. If they rejected her, she had nothing left.

However, Abby benefited in one way by moving to the Home. They arranged for her to attend a junior college and allowed her to live with them until she graduated. Her grades were good, and she buried herself in her lessons. Books became her primary companion.

After graduation, Abby moved back to Jonesboro, but by that time, she no longer fit in there either. Her prior friends developed new relationships and they no longer included her. Some moved away and several married. *"You can't ever go back home,"* she often told herself. *"But then it doesn't matter because I don't really have a home to go to".*

Abby found a job at Simmons Bank and rented a small apartment. She developed a casual friendship with co-workers and frequently spent time with one of them on weekends. This friend, Sandra, seemed no more outgoing than Abby, but she was a smart dresser and took Abby under her wing and taught her fashion techniques. They occasionally went to Memphis just to shop and eat at some place different.

Abby credited her solitary life as the primary reason she taught children at church. Her class of four-year-olds played a dominant role in her life. She liked preparing their lessons and loved every one of the children. She tended to treat one or two to lunch after worship on Sundays. Abby wanted to feel closer to them. With a child, she felt safe and needed. She laughed and acted silly as if she were their age.

CHAPTER FOUR

RAPID ROMANCE

N ot only did Connor send Abby red roses, but he phoned her promptly at 8:00 pm that Monday evening. They talked for almost an hour. She wanted to ask how he knew to send thirteen flowers but feared to ask might indicate her lack of social skills because she had no idea why such a thing mattered.

Connor phoned every night afterwards and his weekend visit developed into numerous weekend visits. They ate at practically every restaurant in Jonesboro, and he took her to Memphis many times. There they visited the zoo, toured several museums, and Elvis' estate. They ate enough bar-be-cue to begin looking like pigs.

Connor taught Abby new things about Little Rock, and she appeared excited to have a personal story to share with him about Memphis, specifically about Elvis Presley. Connor had not visited Elvis' estate before, and she had a private tidbit of information about Elvis that few knew.

As they walked up the long drive to Elvis' home, Abby's excitement grew. "My mother was almost tempted to go out with

Elvis," she said with a giggle. "Mother bragged about it and told the story every opportunity she had. I loved hearing her tell it because of how excited she always became. Her eyes twinkled every time she related what happened. Her love of Elvis became a family tale, and Daddy bought her songs, posters, and every type of Elvis memorabilia he could find. I still have her collection and cherish it. Just visiting here brings back good memories because she and I came here several times together."

"So, what happened?" asked Connor.

"As Elvis worked to increase his popularity, he played in many small towns. He and others like Johnny Cash played in Bono High School, a small community about ten miles north of Jonesboro. The seniors scheduled them to play, charged admission, and used their share of the ticket money to take a senior trip. Mother's friend attended school in Bono, and she invited mother to go with her to see Elvis. After his performance, mother raced to join the line of girls, asking for Elvis's autograph. She was seventh in line. Elvis asked each girl if he could drive her home. The girls, numbers one through five, turned Elvis down, but number six accepted. Had she refused like the others, he would have asked my mother."

"Would she have gone with him?"

"No way! My grandmother would have killed her. Nice girls didn't date musicians back then. That is why numbers one through five refused. So you can imagine how my mother described the girl in front of her. It's just the thrill she would have enjoyed by being able to say that she was asked out by Elvis Presley."

"But that's not all the story. It seems some of the school boys followed Elvis. He took girl number six to a nice restaurant, ordered pie and ice cream, and drove her directly home. He walked her to the door, kissed her on the cheek, and left. Mother always imagined being kissed goodnight by Elvis. So Daddy bought her tons of Elvis things and always said Elvis was the only man who could have beat him for mother's hand. He used to wink at me and say if Elvis had been my father, I'd be rich today."

"They held Elvis' event in the school gymnasium. Mother said the gym bleachers were packed, the floor overflowed with folding chairs shoved together, and people stood leaning against the walls. People who couldn't crowd inside, sat on the porches and stood outside just to listen. Mother was thrilled to have a seat near the front and be that close to Elvis. But Elvis was their last performer. After his performance, the school enacted a rule that banned all musical groups. When Elvis finished playing, there was such a mob trying to get close to him and the band that the gym floor cracked and a long section of hardwood needed replacing. So, Elvis was their last great performer. But he packed the house."

"Daddy always bragged about Elvis being his biggest rival. He teased mother by saying, "If I was going to end up in second place, at least it would take a celebrity to beat me.""

CHAPTER FIVE

GETTING TO KNOW YOU

O f all their outings, Abby enjoyed Memphis zoo the most. That day, she admitted how much she liked being with Connor.

Connor stopped at a convenience shop and purchased a couple of apples, package of peanuts, and box of crackers. "It's to feed the elephants and birds," he explained.

In the elephant house, Connor forced Abby to hold the apple. "Come on take the apple. Let Bozer eat it from your hand. He won't hurt you." Connor took Abby's hand and placed the apple in it.

"He sure smells bad. Actually, he stinks," Abby said. "He needs a bath, not an apple."

"Do you want me to find a water hose and let you bath him?"

"I don't think the quick shop sells that much soap," laughed Abby, as Bozer lifted his trunk toward Abby and brushed her arm. Abby squealed and dropped the apple. Bozer swiped her arm again, as if to punish her for dropping it. Both of them laughed as Connor chased the apple.

At Monkey Island, one monkey swung to the edge of the water and began chatting as if he was trying to talk to them. Connor repeated a similar sound. The monkey spoke again, and Connor repeated a noise that matched the monkey's as closely as he could.

"Seems you two have a thing going," laughed Abby. "Let's see if we can toss him a cracker." The monkey loved the attention, and soon other monkeys joined him. He reached into the air with each toss, but few made it that far. The few he did catch brought more chatter from him, followed by Connor's mimicking attempts.

As they were leaving, Abby admitted to Connor, "This is the most fun I have had since my parents died. I feel young again. I think I have felt 80 years old since the day I learned they were dead. I often wished I had been with them and died too. In a way, I guess I did. I know that a piece of my heart and emotions died with them. Sometimes, I wake at night and I can still smell the carnations atop their casket. Today I only smelled the elephant. Stinky as he was, it was nice. Thank you for today. You made me laugh. I don't feel afraid to have fun with you because you seem relaxed no matter where you are. I can't explain it, but it's like today's my first real day to live again and to genuinely want to live. Not sure if it's you or the animals or both, but it's been a wonderful day."

"And it's not over, pretty lady," interrupted Connor. "I plan to stuff you full of bar-be-cue before we leave. I noticed a sign on our way here that advertised bar-be-cue and karaoke. We'll eat there and sing at the top our lungs. Who cares if others laugh? We are going to enjoy the evening and not waste a minute of our time together."

Abby laughed as freely with Connor as she did with her four-year-old church friends, and with good reason: Connor's singing sounded terrible. Apparently he was tone deaf, but he didn't care. He bellowed out so loudly that Abby covered her ears. *"If he doesn't care, then neither will I,"* she thought. The music blared loudly and others couldn't actually hear them, but Connor wouldn't have cared if they did.

Abby decided Connor's openness was what captured her. He acted as he wanted in public. He didn't worry about what others thought, and more importantly, he told her personal things about himself. He shared the type of things she tended to keep private.

He explained how his father died following a sudden heart attack as he drove home from work. During the attack, the car plowed into a tree and was totaled. Fortunately a police car drove by, and they phoned for an ambulance. Ten days later, his dad died in the hospital.

His mother suffered a stroke the following year and died at home in her sleep. Shocked to discover his mother dead, Connor ordered an autopsy. He learned that she experienced a series of small strokes before this big one, but he never knew. She showed no recognizable sign of other strokes. Her memory began to fail, but he attributed it to her age. He experienced guilt about missing the early signs until a friend asked what he could have done to stop them if he had known.

Like Abby, Connor hated being an only child. He had a younger brother who died at six weeks of age, and Connor often wondered what their life would be like if the brother had lived.

Connor attended Stanford and graduated with a law degree but immediately returned to Little Rock to help his father in their investment business. He talked about his social life at Stanford and his stressful readjustment moving back to Little Rock.

The only information Connor didn't share was life with his dead wife, Emilie, or her family. Apparently, at least for now, that part appeared off limits.

Abby could not believe Connor revealed private information that she considered taboo about her own life. She needed to know a person years before sharing such personal details. Few co-workers even knew that her parents were deceased.

At Connor's insistence, Abby took him to visit the Children's Home in Paragould and introduced him to the house parents. Her face burned fire engine red when they told Connor she was their pride and joy. They insisted that not all their children develop into such beautiful adults. After touring the grounds, Abby took Connor's hand and pulled him towards the car. She insisted she needed to leave. Being there brought back too many memories of being lonely and feeling abandoned.

On the drive home, Abby explained to Connor why she pushed to leave. "While living at the Home, I experienced the same recurring nightmare several times a week. I would see my parents in their car and a long 18-wheeler headed toward them. I cry out to them to stop or pull over, but they don't hear me. I always woke screaming and crying. The salty taste of my tears brought back visions of my parent lying in their caskets and how I cried seeing them. I laid awake hours trying to make myself think of something else, but the more I tried, the more I cried. I continued dreaming this until I moved back to Jonesboro. There the dream stopped. I wanted to leave and be forced to think about something else. I couldn't bear remembering that dream."

Connor pulled to the side of the road and held Abby closely for several minutes. "Thanks for telling me," was all he said. For Abby, that proved more than enough.

Connor also insisted on touring Arkansas State where Abby took an evening class. He wanted to know every detail of her life. She showed him her classroom, and he plopped down in the chair where she usually sat. He asked her to describe what proved the most difficult for her to learn and pretended to understand. She knew he didn't, but liked that he wanted to know.

The place Abby felt most comfortable taking Connor was to worship services at her church, especially after he explained that he grew up attending one of the same faith. Connor admitted, "I changed churches to please my ex-wife. She insisted on attending a much larger one of a different faith. Size mattered to her. I like that you go to the one I attended as a youngster. It's where I feel at home. I never felt quite right going to her choice, but she insisted, and I caved and tagged along. I think that's what God means by not being unequally yoked. We were never aligned in our beliefs. I put her requests first and put second how I believe the Lord wants us to worship. I agreed to keep peace. I didn't admit this until I went to church with you. I want you to know that I repented of that sin and promised God I won't ever do that again."

Connor's honesty and ability to speak so vulnerably always shocked Abby. She wished she could share like that with others or at least with him.

Connor remained in the auditorium Bible class while Abby taught her four-year olds. Afterwards, they sat near the back, with a different child from her class each week. Connor enjoyed sharing Sunday lunch with Abby and the children. He seemed to enjoy the children even more than Abby did, and she liked that.

Abby carried a bath towel and large pin in the car so they could take the children for ice cream. She wrapped the towel around their necks and ordered them a double dip topped with extra sprinkles. The large towel proved good protection for their nice clothing. They could make a mess, and their parents wouldn't care. Connor always told the children he wished she would bring him one too which made them laugh. Afterwards, they went to the park and argued about who swung the highest.

The following week, Connor insisted they should invite Sandra, her co-worker friend, to spend the day with them. Connor didn't want to cause Sandra to spend every weekend alone, now that he dominated Abby's time. At first, Abby hesitated. She expressed concern about others knowing so much about their relationship, but Connor insisted. "I want her to know how much I like being with you." Abby blushed and stopped arguing.

Sandra refused their invitation. She insisted she needed to help her sister with wedding plans. She told Connor that she never liked being a third wheel, and unless he had a good-looking brother to bring along, she couldn't risk offending her sister by not helping her. However, she did invite Abby and Connor for dinner and agreed to let Abby bring dessert. "It will show him what a good cook you are, especially since desserts are your specialty," Sandra said. Connor brought flowers for Sandra, and they spent the evening sitting at the dining table talking for hours.

Later, Sandra told Abby, "You better grab hold of that man and not let him go. He's a real catch." Her words both embarrassed and pleased Abby. She liked having her best friend's approval.

The ultimate challenge for Abby was Connor's asking to attend her bank's Christmas party. Abby hesitated. She felt torn between wanting to show off Connor and feeling vulnerable over so many knowing more about their relationship. But Connor gave her no choice. He planned to attend and insisted that she open his Christmas present so she could wear it to the event. He gave her a gold chain with a small solitaire diamond pendant. Abby felt awkward wearing such an expensive necklace. She rarely wore jewelry and feared others would notice such an exquisite piece. She would wear it because it was Connor's gift, but she hoped no one asked about it.

As usual, Abby wanted to hang back and stand to the sideline at the party. There were too many attendees Abby didn't know. But Sandra saved her. As others walked nearby, Sandra called to them and introduced Connor as Abby's friend from Little Rock. After that brief introduction, Connor took charge and kept the conversation alive. Smiling was the best Abby could do. She felt proud of Connor, but at the same time, she wanted to hide. She felt terribly uncomfortable. Connor seemed to understand and not care. He could make small talk with strangers as if they were his long lost cousin.

After several months of Connor making trips to Jonesboro, he suggested that Abby should come to Little Rock, stay at his house, and meet his housekeeper, Mrs. Vernon. He assured her that Mrs. Vernon would prove a trustworthy chaperone. He promised to escort her to church, and stressed she could select which one they attended. He would drive her around Saturday and let her see the outside of the buildings. Then she could decide if she wanted to visit a large or small one.

Abby hesitated. She wanted to see where Connor lived but felt uncomfortable at the same time. Finally, she admitted, "Yes, I would like that. In fact, I would like that very much."

Once Abby agreed, Connor divulged that there was something he needed to tell her. "I have a dark, ugly secret from my past. I want to tell you about it, but I can't just yet. I need to feel more comfortable, more solid in our relationship. But I give you my word that at some point I will tell you. I just need to know you won't hate me when I do."

Abby looked surprised. Connor tended to openly discuss so many private topics. Perhaps this proved that he was human after all. Taking his hand, she replied, "I won't hate you, Connor. I promise. I guess everyone has parts of their lives they guard. I know I do. I understand needing time before you share certain things. I tend to hide a lot. So, take as long as you need. When you are ready, I will do my best to understand."

CHAPTER SIX

ANOTHER DIAMOND

Entering Connor's home, Abby gasped. She stood frozen for a minute. Her tiny apartment could fit inside his foyer. Finally, managing to laugh, she asked, "Do you ever get lost and can't find your way out? Or do you drop cookie crumbs as you go?"

Connor explained that his deceased wife, Emilie, designed it. "She liked to hold large parties and wanted a place to show off. I just went along. She was a social butterfly who worked at being with people she considered influential. She learned this from her parents. I became her chaperone to support her preferred lifestyle."

"But being a senator and having a large company, this must have been the support you needed professionally," commented Abby.

"Well, yes. It helped to assure people voted my way."

Connor paused and then his face reddened as he confessed, "I need to share something that I avoided telling you because I find it awkward. Emilie's mother, Mrs. Reed, lives in the small cottage out back. Shortly after Emilie's father died, her mother was diagnosed with early stage Alzheimer's. Emilie decided to remodel the guest house and move her mother into it. That let her care for her mother without moving her into the house with us. Emilie was her only child living in the area, and Emilie was definitely her favorite daughter. Mrs. Reed never hid that Emilie was her favorite, and after Emilie died neither sister offered to care for their mother. One sister lives in Florida and the other in Oregon."

Connor paused before continuing. "After Emilie's death, I didn't know what to do about her mother. I never really liked the woman. Well, actually it's more accurate to say that she never liked me. Anyway, with Mrs. Vernon's help, I found a woman to live with her and just let them continue living in the cottage. Someone needed to ensure she had food and the basics. Really, she just needed someone to talk with so she wasn't alone all the time. However she speaks so rudely to people that it's been very difficult keeping her a companion. I am not convinced that she has Alzheimer's because as long as I have known her she's spoken with a sharp tongue. She's become worse since moving here. I think Emilie moved her to our cottage to avoid her constant complaint about being alone. But Emilie insisted she has early Alzheimer's. So who knows?"

"I admit, she's been through three care-givers so far. They resign saying they can't take her meanness. She called the police on one woman, claiming the woman stole from her, and they discovered her lost necklace in a drawer. So, I avoid her. I live in this house, she lives out back, and we never see each other. You may meet if you want, but I must warn you that she isn't the nicest person."

"Is there a special reason you want me to meet her?" Abby didn't know what to make of Conner's comments. It was the first time he spoke of his ex-wife. Was this the dark secret he promised to tell her? Probably not. This didn't seem something to keep secret from her. Undoubtedly, many people knew this.

"Your choice, but you may want to meet her before the weekend is over. If so, I will introduce you."

"Then meeting her can wait. However, I think I should meet your housekeeper since she is my chaperone for the weekend." Abby smiled as she headed through the doorway to explore the next room.

Mrs. Vernon, the housekeeper, was a tall, matronly widow who walked with her head held high, as if she felt in full command. She rarely smiled. Abby told Connor that her first impression of Mrs. Vernon was, "A woman in total control with an overly serious face that implies you better not challenge her or get in her way."

Mrs. Vernon proved polite enough, but Abby knew it would require real effort to win her as a supportive friend. But, she would work on it. Mrs. Vernon took good care of Connor, and Abby definitely wanted her as a friend.

Abby asked Mrs. Vernon to show her around the house. She could tell the house had several more rooms to see. Mrs. Vernon led the way.

During the tour, Mrs. Vernon pointed to a closed door and explained, "Mr. Connor keeps this room locked. He never goes in. It was Emilie's room, her private space, and nothing has been changed since she passed. I don't think I should open it, unless you insist."

"Oh no, don't do that, Mrs. Vernon. I don't want to intrude on any place that's private." Mrs. Vernon smiled her first smile.

"And please, Mrs. Vernon, call me Abby. I would really like that."
Mrs. Vernon nodded but retained her formal look.

Connor asked Mrs. Vernon to prepare them a candlelight
dinner on the patio. He wanted time alone with Abby. People
chatting noisily in restaurants proved annoying and many paused
to speak as they passed their table. He often thought he couldn't
complete a sentence to Abby without an interruption.

After dessert, Connor asked Abby to walk to the gazebo
where he surprised her by dropping to his knees and proposing.
Abby stepped backwards. She almost stumbled off the step. He
held the largest diamond she had ever seen. "But Connor, we've
only known each other a short time. How can you know me well
enough? Besides, I don't fit in with your social life. I am shy and
reserved, definitely not a social butterfly. Remember, I am a lowly
bookkeeper who lives in a tiny apartment."

"You fit in with the life I want. You are honest, genuine, and I
love you. We can spend the rest of our lives learning the other
parts. I do want you to say yes. I love you and want to spend my
life making you happy."

"I love you too, Connor. I've known it since the second week
we met. But it's so soon. What will others say?"

"What we do is no one else's business. We answer only to
God and each other. Abby, I love you. Will you be my wife?"

"Yes, Connor, if you are sure. But. . ."

"No buts, pretty one. How about if you stay over Monday
and we buy a marriage license? I don't want to wait. I want to
marry you now. I'd insist that we do it today, if we had the
license."

"But I have to work," Abby protested. Everything moved too fast for her mind to focus on what should happen next.

"I hope you work on being a full-time wife because I want us to have a child as soon as you are ready. I can tell how much you love children. It's been fun sharing lunch with you and a different child every Sunday. Once we have a child, you may want to work full-time on motherhood. But know I wouldn't do anything to hinder you from having a career if that's what you want. It's just that after watching you interact with your kids at church, I am betting you would like a family of your own. Am I right?"

"Yes. Oh, yes. I have always dreamed of having children. That's why I teach my four-year-old Sunday School Class. I love kids. Yes, I would like to have a baby too. In fact, I want more than one. I know what it's like being an only child, and I want to give my child a brother or sister."

"Then that settles it. Call your manager early Monday morning and give a week's notice. I will use the week to tie up things at work so we can take a long honeymoon. And I do mean long. I want to have you all to myself for at least a full month. Would that be too long? Where do you want to go? You name it, and that's where we will go. What place sounds the most romantic to you?" Connor rattled on without giving Abby a chance to reply. "I want it to be some place where we can stay in bed all week the first week. I can't wait to make love to you. You may come home pregnant, and I would love that."

"Boy! People would definitely talk then," said Abby, as she scrunched her face. "They would insist that you married me because it was the honorable thing to do for a pregnant girlfriend." Abby wasn't convinced that having a child that soon would prove good timing for Connor's career or for his friends' acceptance of her.

"Okay, if you insist," conceded Connor. "We will wait a few months, but know it's only to save our reputations. Just know that I am fully committed to our relationship and am ready to begin a family the day you say the word."

CHAPTER SEVEN

PRE-WEDDING DOUBTS

A bby grabbed the ringing phone as she dropped her coat on a chair, "Oh, Liddy, hi. What a surprise. How did you know? Who told you Connor proposed?"

"The jeweler where he bought your ring told someone, and well, you know how gossip about celebrities spreads. I just want to assure that you know what you are getting yourself into. Being the wife of a politician can be extremely demanding. He works long hours when they are in session, and you will have lots of time by yourself. And remember, you will be responsible for hosting banquets and social events, and that's nothing compared to how many you must attend. It requires a strong woman to handle such a lifestyle. You must always smile and look happy no matter how you feel. Are you prepared for such demands? Can you handle it all? Think carefully about what will be required of you."

"With Connor's help I'm sure I will learn. He tells me I will be his biggest asset. I know I love him enough to give it my best."

"Well then," Liddy said, as she shifted subjects, "I am the person to plan your showers and rehearsal party. I can even take charge of arranging the reception for you. Connor's yard would make a wonderful backdrop for holding a reception. Will you be married at your church in Jonesboro or one in Little Rock? We have some beautiful, large ones. I could arrange a church for you here, since you don't know many people."

"Thanks, Liddy. I do appreciate your offer but we plan to elope. We are inviting no guests. We plan on it being just the two of us. He's been married before, and I have no family but you. I have no father or brother to walk me down an aisle."

"But what about all his constituents who will feel slighted? You must begin your marriage by considering his social status. You don't want to do anything to hinder his career. You must start thinking about what is required of a senator's wife."

"Connor decided to elope, not me. Liddy, I do thank you for wanting to help. You are thoughtful to offer."

"Then I should be your maid-of-honor. What color dress would you want me to wear?"

"Thank you, Liddy, but we want no one else present. Just a minister and the two of us. No parties or showers. Goodness, his house has everything we could ever need. I don't want people shopping and spending for us when we need absolutely nothing."

"So when's the big day?" Liddy pressed to learn more. She wanted the juicy details before others.

"Next Wednesday morning. We will be married and head directly to the airport."

"Where are you going on your honeymoon?"

"We're telling no one. We want time alone without any phone calls or text messages."

"Liddy, I will be in Little Rock Tuesday. Connor hired movers to take all my things this weekend, except clothes that fit in an overnight bag. I am staying with Sandra, my co-worker, and plan to work with my replacement Monday. Then Tuesday I move permanently to Little Rock. How about if I phone you and we plan lunch one day?" Abby said goodbye and hung up, relieved to stop talking with Liddy.

Liddy's comments flooded Abby with self-doubts, *"Why couldn't Liddy be supportive instead of inferring that I won't fit in? Perhaps she's right? Maybe I won't be able to handle the social demands. I don't know anything about hosting big events. I've never even attended a cocktail party. Maybe I don't know how to do what's required."* Fortunately, Sandra bolted through the door and distracted Abby from her thoughts.

By dinner time, Sandra noticed that Abby seemed quieter than usual and asked what was wrong. Abby required a full hour of them discussing how Connor's actions proved he loved her and that Liddy was mistaken about Abby being the right woman for Connor's life before Abby dismissed Liddy's negative challenges. Sandra insisted that Abby made the right decision and was the perfect type of supportive wife Connor needed. "I do hope others think so too," said Abby as she slowly changed the subject.

CHAPTER EIGHT

CURIOUS ABOUT EMILIE

C onnor spent Tuesday morning changing his banking to Simmons Bank. He thought it might please Abby. Besides if they ever experienced a problem, she would know the right person to contact to correct it. Then he met with his attorney to change his will. Abby arrived in time to meet him for lunch, and Connor asked her to stop by his attorney's office and sign some papers before going home – to their house.

"Besides I want you to meet Charles," explained Connor. "He's not only my attorney, he's my closest friend. I told him all about you, and he can't wait to meet you."

At Charles' office, Abby took advantage of having an opportunity to hear an outsider's opinion and asked, "What was Connor's wife, Emilie, like? How would you describe her? I've never even seen a picture of her."

Charles paused. He stared at Abby for several seconds before answering. "Well, she was pretty. Outgoing. A super sharp dresser, and she loved throwing parties. She was an outstanding hostess."

He paused again as if trying to measure his words. "Yet, Emilie seemed rather aloof. Can't quite put my finger on it, but I never felt I really knew her, not the real her. I am close with Connor but never felt close to her, and I hated that. I would have loved being her friend too. She seemed selective about whom she let know what she really thought. She befriended everyone, and it appeared that others enjoyed her company. She always smiled; yet, I never saw behind her smile. She played the social game skillfully and became a supportive partner with whichever political party held office."

"How could she do that?" Abby asked. "I mean how could she support both Republicans and Democrats without offending some?"

"She learned how from her parents," Charles explained. "You see, her mother was an active Democrat and her father a strong Republican. They supported both parties and attended each other's events. Emilie grew up attending special occasions with both groups. She knew the who's who of both parties."

Charles hesitated again. "And, of course, with her money, she found ways of ensuring she made the guest lists of both parties. After every election, she supported the winner. I handled her affairs and after each election, she sent a large check to the winner, and she didn't care which party the person represented. I read a couple of her notes. She told them she wanted to ensure they could meet the promises they made and hoped her contribution helped. Her large checks guaranteed that she received invitations to their special events. Her family is rich and money allowed them to play both sides of the fence, so to speak. Because of her parents, she knew the right people on both sides."

Both sat quietly for a few minutes before Charles asked, "Why do you ask? Why not ask Connor?"

"I wanted an outsider's opinion," explained Abby. "I was just curious. Since, I will be living in the house she built. I wanted to know more about her. That's all."

"I hope you will be my friend", said Abby. "I have no friends here and would like it if we were good friends."

"Then we will be, Abby. You will love my wife too. She never cared for Emilie. We invited her and Connor for dinner a couple of times, but we just never clicked as couple friends. My wife said Emilie didn't want a close friend. That she didn't want to invest enough work to feel close to a friend. But my wife's going to like you a lot."

After talking with Charles, Abby couldn't wait to go home – to her new home. As she walked in the door, the telephone was ringing. Mrs. Vernon handed the phone to Abby saying it was someone named Liddy. Abby rolled her eyes. *"Not again. Not this soon,"* she thought.

"Listen Abby, I have a great idea. Once you guys return home, why don't I throw a little announcement party. Three hundred people or so. May I? Inviting the right people would help boost Connor's career, you know."

"I am not sure, Liddy. That's something I need to discuss with Connor. However, I can tell you that I would not want that many. How about 50 or less? Could you narrow the list to the minimum necessary?"

"Only if Connor insists." Liddy's tone shifted and revealed her disappointment. "Maybe we could compromise and meet in the middle. Talk with him and let me know. I need to book the hotel room as soon as possible. Do you promise? And remember, you need to meet his friends right away and show that you plan to support Connor. You need his friends to accept you, and I am just the person to help you do that."

Abby sighed, "Okay, I promise to ask him. But you won't hear from me until we return. Please, don't do a thing until I call. And I am not saying when that will be. We agreed to keep our trip a secret. No one knows where we're going or when we will return."

"What about Mrs. Vernon?"

"Connor told her to take a few weeks off with pay. But she insisted she didn't have any place to go or any place she would rather be than here. So, we don't know what she plans."

"What about his mother-in-law, Mrs. Reed? Does she know? I understand that she still lives on the grounds. What will happen to her?"

"For now, she's staying in the cottage out back. I haven't met her yet. I will do that after we return from our honeymoon. Right now, my thinking about her is a very low priority."

CHAPTER NINE

THE BITTER TONGUE

Back from their honeymoon, happy and feeling secure, Abby decided she could handle Liddy and Connor's ex-mother-in-law, Mrs. Reed. This was her home now, and she was the woman of the house. Yes, she could take on anyone. Or so she hoped. Besides, now that she and Mrs. Reed lived on the same grounds, it seemed time for them to meet.

Abby walked to the cottage, took a deep breath of reassurance, and rang the doorbell. When a tall slender woman opened the door, Abby heard a voice calling from inside. "Who is it? Who's there? Well, tell me! What's taking so long? What's wrong with you? Can't you open the door and see who it is?" Abby knew whose voice it was. Connor was correct. Mrs. Reed was not the nicest person. Abby hoped it was just Alzheimer's.

Abby introduced herself to the woman at the door and then headed towards the voice. "Hello, Mrs. Reed. I am Connor's new wife, Abby. I wanted to meet you since we will both be living on the grounds."

"New wife!" Mrs. Reed's shock showed. "Tell me you are kidding!" she screamed. "Connor shouldn't be getting married. My dear Emilie hasn't been gone long enough for him to think about other women. What did you do? Trick him into marrying you? You can't have known him long. Was he cheating with you while my Emilie was alive?"

Abby took a deep breath and tried to appear in control. "I understand it seems fast to you. And no, I only met Connor a few months ago. I didn't know Emilie, but I am sure she was a lovely woman." Abby refused to act defensively. She held her thoughts. She needed to remember that this woman was sick. She refused to allow Mrs. Reed to cause her to feel bad.

"Do you live in Little Rock? What do your parents do? Do you always dress like that? Did Connor marry you to further his career now that my Emilie is gone and he must do it on his own?" Mrs. Reed barked a string of questions without waiting for Abby's reply.

Abby explained briefly the little about herself that she felt comfortable sharing with Mrs. Reed. Unfortunately, even a mini-condensed version of her history proved difficult. Abby wanted to turn and flee, not respond. Instead, she bit her tongue and explained where she used to work and live as nicely as she could.

"You don't really think a bookkeeper can plan all the social events for a man's career like Emilie did, do you? My precious Emilie gave the most wonderful parties. Without them, Connor wouldn't be a senator. Surely you don't think your background prepared you to help advance his career. I can't imagine how a bookkeeper envisions herself as First Lady of our state."

"I shall do my best to support Connor, Mrs. Reed. Perhaps you could give me some pointers when the time comes." Abby felt tears gathering in her eyes. She took Mrs. Reed's words personally and let them upset her.

"You obviously need more help than I have time to give you, young lady. Besides, I am too old to tutor you. You'd never become like my Emilie anyway. My Emilie was the finest. Her social skills made Dear Ann look crude. I regret I can't say the same about Connor."

Abby froze. She couldn't believe that Mrs. Reed was going to talk badly about Connor after all he did for her. But Mrs. Reed ignored Abby's look and continued, "Poor Emilie did her best to make their marriage work, but Connor just used her to advance his career. Lucky for him, Emilie agreed to play the loving wife in spite of how he treated her or he wouldn't be where he is today. Bless her heart, she used to go to their cabin at the lake every weekend to avoid Connor. That meant she couldn't be with me all weekend, but she did what she felt forced to do."

Finally, Mrs. Reed's berating Connor proved more than Abby could handle. Abby clenched her fists so tightly that her fingernails dug into her palms as she tried not to let her anger show. She could take Mrs. Reed's rudeness to her but not her degrading Connor. Abby wanted to tell her how mean she behaved by talking badly about the only person willing to see that she received good care. Instead Abby reminded herself, *"I won't digress to her level. She's a sick woman,"* and replied, "I know you loved your daughter very much. She must have been the joy of your life."

"You bet she was! She proved a better wife than Connor did a husband. Without her, Connor would be a no-body today. I will never forgive Connor for my sweet daughter needing to leave me alone on weekends. Poor thing, she spent practically every weekend on their boat by herself. She lived such a lonely life. Connor pushed her away. You will see. You will learn what a cold and heartless man Connor is."

Abby choked on Mrs. Reed's words and could swallow no more. She knew she needed to leave or she might just slap the woman, even if she did have Alzheimer's. She said her goodbyes and hurried for the door. "I am now in the big house. If I can assist you in any way, do let me know."

"You can't do anything for me. You could never take my Emilie's place. No one can." Mrs. Reed barked at Abby.

"Oh, no. Of course not. I wouldn't try, but if you need something, do call." Abby slammed the door as hard as she could, and immediately felt a twinge of shame for doing so. She rushed outside. How good it felt to smell fresh clean air.

"That poor selfish woman." thought Abby. *"How miserable she must be. How sad to feel so empty and lonely that she fills herself with hate. It's like she's angry at the world. I do hope it's Alzheimer's and not the true her. Besides, she's wrong. Connor isn't at all like she said. I married a good man."* Abby knew Mrs. Reed was mistaken about her new husband.

Abby decided not to tell Connor everything Mrs. Reed said. After all, he did more for her than her other daughters. He ensured she received good care and still she talked about him as if he's a monster. Alzheimer's or not, Abby decided that the poor woman really was sick.

CHAPTER TEN

THE ANNOUNCEMENT PARTY

Liddy insisted on hosting Abby and Connor an announcement party. Her idea of a compromise included 150 guests, none Abby knew. Liddy remained adamant that every person on the list was someone Connor needed to invite. The guest list consisted of his co-workers and people who contributed large donations to his campaign. She coached Abby on what to wear and insisted that she memorize the guest's names. If she associated a wife's name with the wrong husband, it would prove a disastrous social blunder. Abby felt as if she were back in middle school and being threatened that she would never be promoted to high school if she erred.

Liddy took total charge. "I made you an appointment with my beauty salon for a facial, hair styling, and manicure. Afterwards, I will take you shopping and help you select the right formal. Oh yes, and shoes. Shoes are extremely important in this city. The shoes you wear will be noticed by every woman. You must look the part. What you say and how you look can help determine if Connor becomes our next governor, perhaps even president one day. Remember those attending consist of the very ones who helped catapult Clinton into office. But don't worry. I will see that you do everything correctly."

Abby hated being treated this way and tried to convince herself that Liddy was genuinely trying to be helpful. Yet, she felt demeaned. Was her style of dress that wrong? Were her manners and social graces so terrible? Perhaps she wasn't cut out for this new role after all. But she appreciated that Liddy included a massage. Being around Liddy raised her stress level so high, she needed something to help her relax.

Liddy showed the party menu to Mrs. Vernon for her approval. Mrs. Vernon helped plan all of the parties Emilie used to host. Abby admitted that she felt relieved not to have to deal with food too. However, she wondered if Liddy knew how to host a small, informal luncheon with people you were close to or if she always floated with high energy to try to impress others. "Perhaps I will learn, but I do hope I never become this up tight." Abby said softly beneath her breath. Still, Liddy was doing a superb job with the arrangements. Abby did not need to worry if things would go perfectly.

The party was Abby's first black tie event. Her hands trembled. What if she forgot someone's name or called them the wrong name? Connor hugged her and assured her that she would be the queen of the ball. He told her repeatedly how proud he felt to introduce her as his wife and insisted others would love her as much as he did. He bragged about how beautiful she looked.

At the party, things went smoothly for the first hour. Then Connor left Abby's side to mingle with some men. That left Abby alone to talk with the women and the few men who stood to the side. She had never been good at talking with women she didn't know. She did better talking with men about finances. She knew numbers and could discuss them all day, but few women showed any interest in them.

She decided to ask about the women's children. Surely, all women liked to discuss their kids. If asked, she would admit she and Connor wanted children. She made it past two women who seemed comfortable discussing their children before Liddy moved to her side and shifted all talk to politics. Abby felt like a political dunce. She stood smiling and nodding as if to agree with everything Liddy said, but remained silent.

During their drive home, Abby shared with Connor how uncomfortable she felt trying to discuss politics. She explained how she simply spent the rest of the evening in silence and let Liddy do all the talking.

Connor didn't understand. "Couldn't you find something to discuss? They are my friends, and I do want you to like each other. Just speak up and talk with them. I promise they will love you."

"I didn't want to risk embarrassing you, Connor. I feared I might say something wrong and it reflect badly on you. I would never want to do that."

Connor brushed her comment aside and insisted that the more times she was with the people, the more comfortable she would feel. He told her to forget it, but she felt hurt. Abby yearned for a response of support for how she handled the situation, but none came.

"Connor, I probably should tell you something else." Abby spoke slowly, as if testing to see if it was safe to say more. "I really didn't feel comfortable with your vice president, Stanley. I can't quite put my finger on it, but Stanley spoke rather sharp with me twice, almost as if he resented me for something. Or maybe he disapproved of something I did. Anyway I felt very uncomfortable with the way he spoke to me. He wasn't exactly mean, but he wasn't kind either. His tone disturbed me as much as his words."

"Ignore it, Abby. Stan's that way. He tends to answer everyone rather bluntly. He doesn't mean anything by it. You just have to get used to him. He's short with everyone."

"But he really was rude, Connor."

"Please, Abby. Forget it."

It was the first night since their wedding that Connor didn't cuddle her when they went to bed. Abby feared she committed a real social blunder and he was upset with her, but she said nothing. What else could she say? Connor appeared to defend the one man who spoke bluntly – no mean – to her.

The following morning, Abby woke to the phone ringing. Liddy called to ask to host a second announcement party and hold it in Jonesboro. She insisted that expanding Connor's contacts would prove valuable for his career. Surely Abby wanted all her friends to meet Connor, and the more exposure he had, the better his chances of becoming governor. Perhaps, they should also think about a party in Paragould where she graduated high school.

CHAPTER ELEVEN

SOCIAL DISASTER

C onnor phoned Abby from the car. "I'm headed home to change clothes. We need to attend a Dillard fund raising event for a charity organization I support. It's already 4:00 and the invitation says it begins at six. I missed seeing the invitation when we returned from our honeymoon and didn't know about the affair until minutes ago. Can you be ready on short notice?"

"I will try, Connor," Abby said with a strong sense of disappointment in her tone. "I don't do too well with such short notices, but I will try. Am I to wear a formal? How long until you're home?"

Abby ran to find Mrs. Vernon. She needed help. She owned nothing appropriate to wear. She couldn't wear the gown she wore to their announcement party. Many of the same people would be attending. Liddy would die if she thought Abby considered such an idea. For a first time, she wished Liddy was in charge of her attendance at this event too, but obviously, Liddy didn't know about this one.

Mrs. Vernon studied Abby for a few minutes. Her eyes scanned her up and down before she answered. "Come with me,

Miss Abby. I think you fit some of Emilie's gowns. She owned many and never wore the same formal twice. They all still hang in her closet. None of her clothes have been moved."

Abby followed Mrs. Vernon to the upstairs bedroom. Her eyes widened when Mrs. Vernon unlocked the door. Abby had never seen such an elegant room. "It looks like a picture on the cover of a magazine. This room is magnificent." was all Abby could say. Mrs. Vernon did not answer. She led Abby to the huge over-sized closet. Inside the closet, Abby muttered, "My apartment wasn't this large." Mrs. Vernon pretended not to hear.

Mrs. Vernon pulled a gorgeous white silk and chiffon dress from the rack. A single row of tiny red roses ran from the right side of the neckline down to the opposite side of the hem with a red rhinestone shining in the middle of each flower. The gown was the most beautiful dress Abby had ever seen. "Of all her gowns, this was my favorite," explained Mrs. Vernon.

Mrs. Vernon helped Abby slip into the gown and tugged it tighter at the bust. "If I tack it in this area, it will fit you perfectly," assured Mrs. Vernon. "Take it off, and I will have it ready in a second. I'm a pretty good seamstress. You do your makeup, and I will have it mended by the time you are ready. I hear Mr. Connor in the driveway now. I'll tell him that you will be down in a few minutes."

After making the alterations, Mrs. Vernon zipped Abby into the dress. "I have never felt this elegantly dressed before. Do you think it's too much for me?" asked Abby, as she twirled around twice. Mrs. Vernon smiled, pleased that Abby liked the results.

Abby walked halfway down the stairs, when Connor turned to see her. He froze. His smile turned to a frown. His face reddened. Taking a deep breath, he shouted at Abby, "Take that off! What do you think you are doing? Take off that dress this minute! You can't go wearing that. I am leaving. I will go without you. I will explain to everyone that you are busy unpacking your things." Connor stomped out and slammed the door.

Abby stood silently, unable to move for several seconds. What had she done wrong? Tears ran down her cheeks. She turned and raced to her bedroom and flung herself across the bed. Did Connor hate her? Did he resent her wearing Emilie's dress? That must be it. He protected Emilie's things all these years and tonight she invaded that privacy. No, worse. She flaunted something he tried to keep private. How stupid could she be? She made the one unforgivable blunder she would never forget. How could she do this?

Mrs. Vernon knocked on Abby's bedroom door. "Go away, please, Mrs. Vernon. I can't talk now. I was such a fool."

"But, child, it was my idea, not yours. I want to apologize." Mrs. Vernon ignored Abby and slipped inside the door. She walked to the bed where Abby lay sobbing. "I should have known better, Miss Abby. It was my idea, not yours, and I will tell Mr. Connor. He should be angry with me, not you. You only wore the gown because I suggested it. Please, please, forgive me."

"You are not to blame. It wasn't your fault. You tried to help. I made the decision to wear it, not you. I should have said no."

Abby pretended she was asleep when Connor returned home. Connor tiptoed to bed and lay with his back to her.

CHAPTER TWELVE

THE FIRST ARGUMENT

"Connor, I want to apologize for last night. I only thought about myself and being accepted. I gave no thought to how you might feel if I wore something that belonged to Emilie. I promise never to do anything like that again. Please, forgive me."

Connor stiffened. His face turned stern. "Abby, if you want out of our marriage, maybe we could have it annulled. We haven't been married that long. If we can't, I will sign and agree to anything you want in a divorce. You can be free to find someone you can really love."

Abby froze. *"What did he mean? Annulled? Divorced? Surely what happened wasn't that bad."* Abby knew she had done something that met Connor's disapproval but wearing his ex-wife's dress wasn't bad enough to cause a divorce.

Distraught, Abby said, "I don't want out of our marriage. I want to learn what you expect of me, so I please you. I love you and want to be a good wife. I don't want a divorce. But it was your first thought, so you must want out? Is that it?" Abby started to cry. Her hands trembled as she slumped back into the chair.

Connor continued with the same degree of firmness. "It's okay, Abby. I understand. You don't respect me or my friends and don't want to live my lifestyle. I can live with that, but I can't live with a wife who enjoys flaunting it in front of others."

Abby wheezed. Her mind raced, "*What? What did Connor mean? Flaunting what?*" Then she asked, "How does my blunder disrespect you? By wearing your ex-wife's gown? I told you I will never do that again? How can wearing another's gown be bad enough to justify a divorce? I don't get it. How can I make it right?"

"By leaving, Abby. I can't go through this again. I can't live like that. I am sorry. I really thought you were different. In fact, your difference is what I found so attractive. But I can't go through all this again. Please, just decide what arrangements you want and I will agree."

Abby's hurt shifted to anger. "No, Connor! I won't leave you. I love you and want to right the wrong. I want to be the wife you want. Just tell me how. Was it the dress? If so, I told you I won't make that mistake again. What can I do to make things right with you, Connor? I refuse to leave you. I will never divorce you. I am married to you for the rest of my life. I intend to keep that commitment. The only way you can get rid of me is for you to file for a divorce. Even then, you will have to put me out of the house. I am committed to staying. So, tell me what I have to do make this right."

Connor's tone softened a little, "I told you. I can't go through this again. I can't live this way."

"Through what, Connor? Tell me! Help me. I don't understand." The more he talked, the more frustrated Abby became.

"You trying to outdo everyone else. You being critical of my friends. You wanting to dress beyond other's means. Flaunting yourself in front of my friends. Smiling to their faces and then degrading them behind their backs. Being a hypocrite like Emilie. That's what."

Abby gasped. She never dreamed Connor thought such things. "Connor, how did I do that? I wore a hand-me-down dress, not something new and spectacular that I bought. I didn't try to outdo others. I wore it because I owned nothing appropriate to wear. I don't own gowns. Remember I grew up in an orphanage and worked in a bank. I never needed formal gowns before we married. I used Emilie's out of desperation. I didn't want to embarrass you by wearing one of my pant suits. Would a pants suit be appropriate at an event where all the other women wear formals? Would that meet your approval?"

Abby buried her face in her hands. What was going on? Connor's reaction made no sense.

Both sat quietly for several minutes. Finally, Abby looked up and slowly in a soft, gentle tone barely above a whisper repeated, "Connor, I will not leave you. I married you for life. I not only promised you that our marriage was for life, I promised God. I won't ever be the one to go back on our wedding vows. If you want out, you will have to physically put me out of this house. When I commit, I commit all the way. I made a mistake and will make others, but I won't leave you when I make one. Nor will I leave you when you make one. I love you and only want to make you happy. I want to live in such a way that makes God proud of our relationship. Now tell me how."

Hearing her soft, earnest plea, Connor felt ashamed. He looked as sad as Abby. "I am sorry Abby. You really do love me, don't you? It's just that . . . well, I treated you badly and you didn't deserve that. I apologize."

"Yes, Connor. I really do love you. I can't imagine wanting a divorce. Our marriage means more to me than some old dress. I want to spend my life making you proud of me. I want to fit in with your lifestyle. I respect all you do and all you stand for. I respect your work with charities, and the fact that you have money and want to use it for helping others. No matter what you think, I was trying to ensure you were pleased with how I dressed. I never thought about upsetting you. I didn't want you to feel ashamed of how I looked."

"I owe you an apology, Abby. You aren't like Emilie. I see that now. In fact, I knew it all along. It's just that when I saw you in that dress it revived some horrible memories. I applied my memories of Emilie to you and knew I couldn't live like that again. I behaved immaturely and was wrong. I know it, and I'm sorry."

Connor paused briefly before continuing, "With Emilie, I lived hurt and embarrassed for so many years that I judged you by her actions. I do love you, and cherish the fact that you seem so different. But, when I saw you in that dress, it was déjà vu all over again. I saw you as my ex-wife the socialite who wanted to outsmart every woman in Little Rock by how she dressed and talked. Emilie lived as a genuine hypocrite."

"But, Connor, I told you, I do not own a gown. At the last minute I didn't know what else to do. I didn't have time to go shopping."

"Of course you didn't. I realize that now. I am sorry for how I reacted." Connor's apology seemed sincere.

Abby lowered her tone to a soft, gentle whisper. "Please, explain to me. Help me understand so I always behave differently. How did Emilie try to outsmart others? Tell me. I never want to make the same mistake."

"You won't. I know that now," replied Connor. "You aren't like Emilie. You see, she lived with the goal of outdoing everyone and constantly complained about others' dress and manners, as if she were a perfect socialite goddess. She wore that dress to our last event hosted by the Dillard's group. She flew to New York to buy it from Macy's, one of Dillard's competitors. She forgot about the charity event until the last minute or she would have flown to Paris to shop, but she let that particular benefit event slip up on her. New York was the best she could do on a week's notice. She insisted that she would show the Dillard women what real socialites wear. Yet, she never dressed better than they did. They are beautiful women and act and dress especially nice. But driving home from that last event together, she degraded them and all the other women's dresses. Then she ranted about the men making crude remarks to her, and that simply wasn't so."

"Wow! No wonder that particular dress bothered you. The same dress for the same hosted event." Abby paused, wiped her eyes, and asked, "My comments about Stanley the other night, about his speaking rudely to me. Was that something Emilie might have said?"

"Definitely. She spoke badly about everyone. To their faces, everyone thought she loved them. If you visited socially with her, you thought she considered you the world's best person, but behind your back you were the pits. I don't think Emilie genuinely liked anyone. And that includes me and her parents. She remained a spoiled, rich kid who never grew up. The only thing she loved was giving money to people who would repay her with attention.

At every event, she worked at having her picture in the newspaper. The first thing she did when entering a room was to locate the photographer."

"But, Connor, Stanley really was curt to me. I didn't make that up. It shocked me for him to speak that way at our first meeting. I don't know him or what he's really like. I know he's your vice president and that's why it surprised me. If it were me, I might be kissing up to the boss's wife, but I would definitely not say something to hurt her. His tone and words shocked me. That's all. I don't care if he likes me, just so you do."

"I love you Abby. I love how genuine and down-to-earth you are. You could wear ragged jeans and a sweat shirt to any of my affairs, and I would be proud to introduce you to others. It's your honest, down-to-earth self that I admire. How you blush over little things is what drew me to you."

"I want to grow old with you, Abby. I really do, and I want you to stay the real you. I promise never to judge you based on Emilie's fake behaviors again. She was as phony as they come. And I promise never to say the word divorce again. That word has been erased from my vocabulary. I promise."

Abby nodded. "I do want you to take pride in how I dress for your events. I want to make you proud. In fact, I will shop for a couple of gowns and cocktail dresses this week. Then I will have one ready for short notices."

"Get it through your head. I am proud of you. What I love is how you are you all the time. You don't put on a show to outdo others. Besides, once we have a child, we won't be attending so many affairs."

"What do you mean?" Abby didn't understand his comment.

"I plan to quit politics once we have a family. I want to be here with you and our children. I want to change diapers, coach little league games, and attend music recitals. I want to study the Bible with you and learn how to teach a children's Bible class. I love that you do that. I am proud that you began immediately teaching a children's class here. Not everyone wants to teach little ones, but you do, and I like that. Once we have children, I want to take an active role in their lives, not be out trying to change the world. I want to help shape the world of our children. I believe when you shape your children's life, you do more for shaping the world than any politician can ever do."

Abby started tearing again, as she moved to sit in Connor's lap.

CHAPTER THIRTEEN

CHARITY PARTY

By the time Abby woke the following morning, Connor had left for work. Mrs. Vernon explained that Connor told her to clear out all of Emilie's things. She was to give away all her clothes, draperies, linens, furniture, everything, and ask Abby to redecorate the room. She could even change the carpet if she wanted.

Abby liked the idea, but she didn't want to act this fast. "Please, Mrs. Vernon. Don't do that until I can talk with Connor. I want to think about it. Emilie owned such beautiful things. I want to ensure they go to people who will appreciate and use them. I can't imagine dumping them into a Goodwill container in some grocery store parking lot. Give me a few days before you do anything."

That night at dinner, Abby told Connor she wanted to plan a charity event by herself and host it in their home. Their foyer seemed an ideal place. She didn't want his help and definitely not Liddy's. She and Mrs. Vernon could handle all the arrangements. She wanted to ensure Emilie's treasures went to people who valued them. Her things were exquisite and should go to girls who otherwise would never have beautiful clothing. Connor protested briefly but realized how important this was to Abby and agreed.

Abby asked Mrs. Vernon to call a lock smith. She wanted the lock on Emilie's door removed and the door left open at all times. She asked Mrs. Vernon to help lay all of Emilie's professional dresses and suits on the bed and to tag each one with its size.

Abby phoned the Social Work Department at the local university and asked if someone could take a letter to the shelter for battered women. Abby knew they kept the address a secret to protect the women, but she wanted assurance that the director received her note. Then she phoned the half-way house for women recently released from prison. She mailed them letters offering to give Emilie's suits to women who were working or looking for employment and could not afford professional attire. She detailed the available sizes and offered to let the people in charge have as many outfits as they needed. By the end of the week, all of Emilie's dresses and suits were gone.

Abby phoned Paragould Children's Home and asked how many junior and senior girls needed formals. She and Mrs. Vernon packed and shipped them immediately.

Abby phoned two local high school counselors and offered to give the remaining gowns to girls who could not afford one. Prom time was just around the corner, and she wanted all the girls to have a gorgeous dress to wear. Wearing Emilie's formals, these girls would stand out like the belle of the ball this year. Abby rented racks and hung the gowns in rows in the foyer.

Three carloads of girls arrived on the appointed day. The girls giggled and cheered as each twirled around displaying the gown of her choice. Even Connor enjoyed watching the girls. He and Abby applauded as each girl modeled the one she wanted. Then he helped fold each gown into a bag.

One gown remained after all the girls retrieved their selection. As they were leaving, one girl stepped close to Abby and whispered, "May I take that one for my younger sister. She will be a junior next year and won't have a formal unless she can have that one. This is the first formal I've ever owned. I didn't attend the prom last year because my mother couldn't afford to buy me one."

Abby hugged her and told her not to move. She hurried to find a large, black plastic zip up bag. She removed the remaining gown from the rack, and tucked it inside the bag. "Take this, honey. I am glad your sister can use it. I am sure she will look beautiful in it. I put my phone number inside the bag. If the gown needs altering, you call me. With Mrs. Vernon's help I am sure we can alter it to fit." The teenager walked away crying as she held a gown folded across each arm.

Abby stood smiling as she watched the girls drive away. "What a beautiful day! Wasn't it wonderful, Connor? Thank you for letting me do this. Next to our wedding day, this may be my best day ever." Connor agreed. He beamed with pride over Abby's idea.

Abby told Mrs. Vernon not to prepare lunch for her and Connor. Mrs. Vernon needed some time to rest. She worked long hours helping Abby empty Emilie's room. Abby and Connor could grab sandwiches because they were going out anyway. Abby planned to take Conner shopping.

Abby wanted Connor to help select hardwood flooring. She planned to turn Emilie's bedroom into a nursery and replace the carpet with a rich colored hardwood. She read that most allergies are caused by dust in carpet, and Abby wanted to ensure they reared healthy children.

CHAPTER FOURTEEN

THE DREADED SECRET

As Abby turned into the driveway, she met two police cars leaving. Panicking, Abby rushed in the house. "Where's Connor? Who's hurt? Mrs. Vernon what's going on? What's wrong? Why all the police?"

"Connor left with the policemen in their car," explained Mrs. Vernon. "They are going to the cabin at the lake. Someone discovered Emilie's boat and found her body inside."

"What? I need to go. How do I find the cabin? I have no idea how to find it?" Abby hurried to the office in hopes of finding a map.

"I will draw you directions as best I can," said Mrs. Vernon as she searched for a pencil and paper. "I was only at the cabin one time. That was several years ago when Miss Emilie hosted an outdoor party at the lake." Abby snatched the drawing from Mrs. Vernon and ran to the car. She hoped she could find it. Her cell phone was dead, and she wouldn't be able to phone Connor for directions.

When Abby arrived at the cabin, the area swarmed with people. She recognized Liddy and a few familiar faces she'd seen before but didn't know their names. Several people moved around taking pictures, and a television reporter stood with her back to the lake describing the episode.

Abby searched for Connor. "What's going on?" she asked.

Whispering, Connor answered, "I will explain later. I don't want to talk where others might hear."

Abby hung back and watched. Liddy moved to hold her hand, but Abby jerked away and crossed her arms. "Connor phoned me when he couldn't reach you," explained Liddy. "He thought I might know where you were. I came immediately here." Abby could not deal with Liddy today. She wanted to watch and listen. She needed to hear what was happening, not talk. Abby walked to the opposite side of the crowd to observe the men working.

Abby watched as the shell of a large boat lifted from the water. A large crane hauled it onto shore. The boat looked black and burned and a hundred years old. The name on the, side of the boat was barely legible. It read 'Emilie's Paint Shop.'

Abby overheard someone saying that some beginner scuba divers discovered the boat during a practice dive. They searched inside and found a body trapped in the barrel of the boat. They contacted the police, and the police arranged for removal of Emilie's remains.

Darkness fell before everyone left, and Abby and Connor were alone. Connor took Abby's hand and led her inside the cabin before he spoke. "I want you to see what it looks like on the inside. We will not come here again. I want to sell it as quickly as possible. It brings back too many horrible memories. I should have sold it a long time ago, but instead, I just pretended it didn't exist. I avoided it and took the easy way out."

Abby wandered through the cabin's three small rooms. The kitchen opened to the living area. Two small bedrooms with a bath between them lined the back. The entire cabin seemed a dramatic contrast from the huge house in town. Still, Emilie's taste in color and décor shone in every room. The cabin appeared almost as nicely done as Emilie's bedroom at the big house, but the rooms were small. Over-sized paintings stood everywhere. A large stack leaned against the wall in the corner, and a few stood atop easels. An open closet door revealed an overflow of paints and stretched canvas. Connor stood quietly watching Abby explore every corner.

"What's that smell?" Abby asked sniffing. "It seems I should know it, but I can't place it."

"It's probably paint thinner or turpentine. Emilie dabbled in paint. She painted all these pictures that you see. She often went out on the boat to paint the lake with the shore line and trees in the background. She wasn't very good but she enjoyed it, and it kept her away from the house in town which I enjoyed."

"Weren't you two close? I told you her mother complained that Emilie visited the cabin almost every weekend." Abby decided it was time she knew more about his relationship with Emilie.

"Not close is a grave understatement. I hate to say this after they just found her body, but Abby, I disliked the woman. The longer we were married the more I resented her. She was wicked."

Connor's harsh words shocked Abby. He never used such word to describe anyone before, not her when she wore Emilie's gown and not to portray Mrs. Reed.

Curious Abby asked, "What? Why? You were married for several years. What was so wrong that you use such strong words?"

"Three and half years to be exact. We were married three and half years," Connor interrupted Abby.

Taking a deep breath, Connor continued. "Abby, we lived separate lives. Once we returned home from our honeymoon we never slept together again. I never so much as touched her again. Not even a small hug. Our first day home, she informed me that we would never again have sex or sleep together. She said she married me to help advance my career. Her only goal was to ensure that I became governor of Arkansas and possibly president one day. When she told me this, I didn't believe she really meant it. I had never heard of such an arrangement. But that day she moved all her things into her bedroom and installed a new lock on the door. A few weeks later, I did go to her door one night. I turned the knob, and she barked for me to go away, saying she wanted nothing to do with me sexually. My ego crashed. I felt ashamed for having made such a bad marriage decision. It was days before I could look her in the eyes. I left the house early and returned home late just to avoid seeing her."

"How could you live like that?" Abby couldn't believe what she was hearing.

"I buried myself in my work. Like I said, at first I didn't think she really meant it. Then the following month, my Dad suffered his heart attack. I felt forced to learn the business as fast as I could. I became a workaholic. Emilie said she would do what was necessary to guarantee my political career. She dreamed of being First Lady, but that was the extent of our relationship. She worked to ensure we received invitations to all the important social events. I tagged along as her chaperone. I convinced myself I was doing good things for the state as I advanced in politics."

"But you were willing to divorce me. Why didn't you divorce her? Why live like that for all that time?" Abby felt a strong tug of jealousy.

"I did it for my father and our business, Abby. Dad started our business with hand-me-downs from his family. He owed a lot of money. Emilie said she and her father would ruin me if I ever challenged her or talked about divorce. And they could. They hold that much influence both politically and financially. Her family would not tolerate a divorce without revenge - serious revenge. To them, divorce implied failure, and their daughter was no failure, at least not in their eyes."

Connor paused. Abby sat quietly. She didn't know what to say. Connor loaded her with unexpected information that she felt unprepared to hear.

Finally, Connor spoke. "Didn't you find Mrs. Reed hostile and obnoxious? Even with possible Alzheimer's, she doesn't compare with Emilie's ruthlessness. Her family would have ruined me and my father. I couldn't let Dad die a broken man because I made a horrible marriage decision. I did what I felt forced to do to protect him and to guard myself. I hated myself for doing it, but at the time, I felt I had no other choice."

Abby interrupted. "Did your parents know?"

"No. It would have destroyed Dad. In public, Emilie and I appeared to live the perfect life, but we had no relationship behind closed doors. That's why I cherish our marriage and couldn't bear the thought that you might ever behave like her."

Abby walked to Connor and put her arms around him. "Oh, Connor, I'm sorry for the years you spent this unhappy. I love you and want you to know that no matter how upset you become with me, I will never sleep in another bed. We belong together. Besides, I really like sex with you. So, let me get this officially on record. You can't avoid sex with me, Mr. Cohen. We belong together in the same bed every night for the rest of our lives."

Suddenly, Abby saw something shiny on the floor sticking out from beneath an end table. She bent to pick it up, but Connor yelled at her, "Stop! Don't touch it! I wanted you to see it, but, please, don't touch it. The knife belongs to the rest of the story that I need to tell you. Once home, I will explain everything. But I need to leave. I can't stand being here long enough to talk more. I will tell you everything at home. I promise. Can we go?"

Abby didn't know what to say. *"More? There's more?"* Already, Connor's story seemed too much to absorb. She felt overwhelmed and wanted to think about Connor's comments before hearing more. Too many of his details seemed disjointed. Too much needed an explanation, but driving home, neither spoke.

Once home, they went directly to their room. Connor wanted to ensure Mrs. Vernon couldn't hear.

Just as Connor and Abby sat on the bedroom sofa, their bedroom door flew open with a loud bang. Shocked, Connor leaped to his feet. Abby gasped. It was Stanley, Connor's vice-president, red faced and cursing. "How could you?" he yelled. "How could you kill her? You didn't deserve her. She didn't love you. She loved me. You murdered her."

CHAPTER FIFTEEN

YOU'LL PAY

Mrs. Vernon trailed behind Stanley apologizing for the intrusion, but Stanley could not be stopped. Mrs. Vernon proved no match for his aggression.

Abby sank into a corner of the sofa. She did not know what was happening, but it obviously meant trouble.

Stanley ignored Abby and continued yelling at Connor. "You killed her! I know you did! You didn't want her having our baby. You low life! I looked inside the boat and saw where Emilie banged and beat on the door. She even cracked the window trying to escape. She painted the word HELP on the boat wall to let everyone know you trapped her. You locked her inside, and she tried to escape. You did this! You drowned her. You killed her! I guarantee that you will spend the rest of your life in prison. You not only killed Emilie, you killed our baby."

Connor interrupted him. "Calm down, Stan. I don't know what you are talking about. Emilie wasn't pregnant. And I did not kill her."

"Yes, she was!" Stanley continued to yell. "Her doctor confirmed it. It was my baby - our baby. You knew it, and that's why you killed her."

"So you are the one she met every weekend at my cabin. Couldn't you even take her to some place of your own? You used my cabin and my boat for your illicit affair. Oh, and by the way, Stanley, you're fired."

"Believe me I was never coming back to the office. I can't work beside a murderer."

"And I can't work with an adulterer. So please, leave. You may have spent many more hours than I have at my cabin, but this house remains my private domain, and you are trespassing. Get out! Get out now or I will call the police and have you arrested."

"You're the one who's going to be arrested!" yelled Stanley, as he headed for the door. He turned to make one last threat. "You will regret this, you useless piece of garbage. I am going directly to the police. I will raise such a stink your career will be ruined. I phoned my reporter friend at the Democrat Gazette, and he loves your juicy story. Your career is ruined! I promise you that."

Abby took a deep breath and stared at Connor. Neither said anything for several minutes. Both felt too shaken.

Finally, Connor spoke. "Abby I am sorry this happened. Perhaps you should go away for a few weeks until this thing settles. In fact, after I tell you what really happened, you may want that divorce."

"I don't want to mix the word divorce with what happened to Emilie. So, stop that talk. Why did Stan accuse you of killing her?"

"Because in one way I did," Connor said softly, as he bowed his head.

"What!" Abby couldn't believe her ears.

"Let me explain." Connor slumped back on the sofa. "Emilie told me the lock on the boat door was not working as it should. She locked herself inside the cabin a few weeks earlier and dug the hinges loose to escape. I drove up late that Saturday afternoon to try to repair it. I phoned ahead to let her know I was on my way. I knew she was having an affair with someone. In fact, I suspected she saw multiple men, but I didn't want to know who they were. We never discussed it because I knew Emilie would claim she did it only to foster my political career."

"Anyway, when I arrived at the cabin she was alone and sitting on the couch. I asked where her lover was, and she jumped up and slapped me. She was furious. She turned and walked to the kitchen. She stood in front of the cabinet a few seconds. Then she opened a drawer and grabbed a knife. She came at me with a butcher knife. Her face glowed with anger. Her eyes widened as big as saucers. You saw the knife. It barely sticks out from beneath the end table. Remember? That's where it landed when she dropped it. When she came at me, I slapped her arm hard to protect myself. She lost her balance and fell backwards. She hit her head on that rough wooden box where she stored paints. She lay very still. For a while, I thought she was unconscious. I stood staring at her for a long time. I finally checked and discovered she had no pulse."

Abby interrupted Connor. "Whoa! Stop! Then it wasn't your fault. It was self-defense. You didn't kill her. It was an accident. You were protecting yourself."

"But Abby, don't you see, it would be my word against a corpse. You saw Stanley. I didn't know the other man was him, but you know from how he acted tonight all the accusations he would make. Even now he thinks I murdered her because she was pregnant. However, I do not believe Stan. Emilie told me the day after our honeymoon that she never wanted children. She said no child would ruin her figure and get in the way of our social life."

"Abby, I couldn't risk being accused of murdering her. There were no witnesses. We were alone. I panicked. I didn't know what to do. I was scared. No, I was terrified! I resented the woman. I hated our relationship. Worst of all, I hated myself for allowing our life to continue that way for all those years. But I didn't want her dead. I felt relieved and terrified all at the same time. I sat on the sofa not knowing what to do. I stared at her body for what seemed like hours. I kept hoping she would move. I wanted her to groan or something to prove she wasn't dead. It was like I sat in the midst of a long nightmare. However, I did have sense enough not to touch the knife. I did think about that. I used my foot and pushed it farther under the table so it was visible only if you stood by the recliner. Finally, all I thought about was doing something with her body and getting out of there."

"But what about the word 'help' on the boat wall?" Abby interrupted, remembering what Stanley said.

"Well, if the police decide to check that, they will find that she has several paintings with words on them. One of her large pictures has the word help at the top, and near the bottom, she painted a picture of a tiny puppy facing an empty bowl. For all I know, Emilie painted the word on the wall months before, possibly to remind her to paint the puppy picture. I don't know. I had not been on the boat in years. But I do know she had no pulse. She couldn't have painted the words that night." Abby nodded in understanding.

They sat quietly for several minutes. Abby reasoned, *"If I were trapped in a sinking boat I would not stop and paint something on the wall. I would be too busy trying to escape,"* but she didn't say it aloud. Connor was too emotional for her to add to his story. She needed to stop questioning him. He might think she didn't believe him. She should let him tell the story his way.

After more silence, Connor continued, "It was almost dark that night and I waited until the neighbor next door couldn't see us. I carried her out to the boat and laid her on the bed. Afterwards, I steered the boat to the middle of the lake as slowly and quietly as I could. I poured her paint thinner around, set it on fire, and ran like a coward. I paddled the dingy to shore on the far side and sank it too."

"I figured everyone would think she caused the fire because she smoked as if there was no tomorrow. I told her several times that she needed to quit, but my suggesting it seemed to make her smoke more. The ashtrays in the cabin overflowed with cigarette butts. The police took them when she disappeared, and they agreed that she probably accidentally set the fire while smoking near her painting supplies."

Abby wanted to find a way to help Connor. She knew he didn't kill Emilie and felt certain that the people who knew him would know it too. Still, there were more unanswered questions. "Didn't the neighbor see you or see enough to know there were two people?"

"I guess not. The neighbors were used to seeing Emilie go out alone in the boat at night. The man next door even phoned me one day at work insisting that my wife should not be alone in a boat after dark. I told him she liked painting sunsets, and when the moon was full, she painted clouds and shadows of the shoreline. That was true. The cabin contained numerous paintings that supported the neighbor's story to the police."

"Apparently it was this neighbor that saw the boat on fire and reported it. By the time the firemen arrived, the boat had sunk.

The policemen phoned to tell me. I was walking in the door when they called. I immediately drove back to the cabin. The following day, they hired divers to search the lake but they couldn't find the boat. I don't know if the man estimated the wrong location or if it floated a while, but they never found it."

"Abby, it took months to have her declared dead. But everyone believed she was dead after the neighbor's comments."

"What are we going to do now?" Abby asked.

"I want to sell the cabin. I hate it almost as much as I hate how I agreed to live with Emilie. I never want to see it again."

CHAPTER SIXTEEN

INVESTIGATION

Mrs. Vernon woke Abby and Connor. "I'm sorry to wake you, but there's a police officer downstairs. He's demanding to speak with you."

Connor dressed quickly and went downstairs. Abby followed in her robe.

The officer wasted no time with small introductions. He wanted to ask his questions and leave. "I'm Detective Goldey. I hate to intrude and so early, Senator, but Stanley Faulkner insists that we investigate the death of your wife. He's making some very strong accusations. We just want to talk with you, and hopefully, put this issue to rest. Where were you the day that your wife disappeared?"

"I was home most of the day. You may ask my housekeeper, Mrs. Vernon. Then I went to the gym to work out, went to a movie alone, grabbed something to eat, phoned Emilie, and came home. The man at the gym desk verified my workout time, and I gave the police my movie ticket stub. When I got the call saying they thought my boat was on fire, I drove to the lake. You should have all that in your records. The police verified my activities at the time."

"Yes, Sir. We have the information. In fact, I was the lead detective, but at that time, there were no accusations of murder. Everyone assumed your wife was alone. After learning the boat served as her artist studio, we thought she accidently set the boat on fire. The ashtrays inside your cabin revealed that she smoked. A chain smoker, I'd say. As I said, we just want to recheck events and put this matter to bed."

"I appreciate you doing that. I would hate to think someone killed her," said Connor.

The officer hesitated and then continued. "Senator, I hate that I have to ask this, but did you know your wife was involved with another man?"

Connor shifted in his chair and blushed slightly. He wondered how many others knew. "My wife and I shared an agreement to live separate lives. I always suspected she was seeing another man, but I never knew for sure. I didn't know with whom until last night when my vice president, Stanley Faulkner, burst into our bedroom upstairs, and said he and Emilie were involved. No. I didn't know they were involved at the time of the fire. If I had, I would have fired him long ago. He definitely would not have continued working for me all this time."

The detective's face reddened as he asked, "Was your wife pregnant, Senator? Do you know?"

"No, I do not. But such an idea shocks me. You see, Emilie never wanted children. She made this very clear early in our relationship. Her mother will confirm that. Emilie's parents used to beg us to have a child, but Emilie wasn't the type to want children. I suggest you go ask her mother. She lives in the small cottage in the backyard."

"Well, that's all the questions I have for now. We have good records from the time of the fire. But I may need to check back later," said the detective as he turned to leave.

"That's fine," replied Connor. "I also want to see her death record permanently closed"

As the officer left, Abby whispered for Connor to come upstairs. She wanted to talk alone.

"Did you really go to a movie by yourself that day?" She wanted to understand Connor's answer because she never attended a movie by herself. For her, going alone seemed strange.

"Yes, I did. I rarely went to movies. They aren't much fun when you have to go by yourself, but it was about the president, and I wanted to see it. My going had nothing to do with Emilie or the fire. I found the movie stub inside my jacket pocket and gave it to the police."

Abby was having trouble putting the pieces together in the right order. "Then when did you drive to the cabin?"

"After the movie. I stopped at a drive through, grabbed a sandwich, and decided to go to the cabin to repair the lock on the boat door. I phoned Emilie from the car. I wanted to give her male friends time to leave before I arrived. Mrs. Vernon confirmed my time at home, and the police accepted my answers, and dropped the matter. They listed it as an accidental fire. After all, how many crazy people do you know who take paints and paint thinner aboard a boat and then smoke like a flaming grill? Her paintings in the cabin supported what I told them and what the neighbor said, as it should because it was all true."

"What will you do now? What do we do?" Anxiety overtook Abby.

"Wait, Abby. Wait is all we can do."

CHAPTER SEVENTEEN

NOT MY DAUGHTER

The police detective took Connor's advice and decided to talk with Mrs. Reed before leaving. He saw no need to make another trip.

When the caregiver opened the door, he practically pushed his way inside. She had firm instructions not to let anyone in without Mrs. Reed's advance approval. But eventually, the officer's badge took priority over her orders.

"I'm sorry to have to be the one to tell you this, but we found your daughter's boat and her body inside. We need to ensure things happened as we originally thought. We are questioning everyone again to ensure all our original ideas prove accurate." He hoped he didn't upset Mrs. Reed.

"I am asking everyone where they were on the day your daughter disappeared. So, can you tell me, where were you?" he asked.

Mrs. Reed took his question as a personal attack, and screamed at him. "You idiot! I was in the hospital with double pneumonia. Afterwards, my daughter's death almost did me in.

You knew that. Two policemen questioned me when they said her boat burned. You should know that!"

"What hospital was that?" The detective asked, as he removed pencil and pad from his pocket to record her answer.

"You idiot. It was St. Vincent. Call them and check. What a foolish question. You should have that in your records. Now, if that's all, you can leave."

"Almost," the detective said, wishing he could leave without asking the next question. "Do you know if you daughter was pregnant?"

"Pregnant! Pregnant? You must be crazy to ask such a question. Emilie hated children. We – my dear dead husband and I - begged her to have a child. We wanted a grandchild but Emilie would not hear of it. She used to say she would kill herself before she risked ruining her figure having a baby. She wasn't about to walk around with a protruding belly as so many women do after giving birth. And she refused to discuss adoption. She insisted if she wasn't having a child of her own, she sure wasn't caring for someone else's."

"So, you are convinced that she wasn't pregnant?" The police detective wanted double confirmation.

"I told you! Yes, I am positive. Detective, my daughter was a wonderful, special person, but she wasn't the kind of woman to care for a baby. Care-giving wasn't her specialty. That's why I needed a full-time woman to live with me. My daughter stayed busy advancing Connor's career and didn't have time or desire to take care of anyone else. She cared about everyone but was unable to care for anyone in an individual way. A lover of all, but a caregiver for none. Ask around and you will see. Everyone loved

Emilie. People used to stop me just to tell me what a lovely person she was. In fact, it's because of Emilie that Connor holds a senate seat. People voted for him because they loved Emilie. Without her, he would not have made it this far. My Emilie was a jewel, but caring for someone else was not her talent. Now if that's all, please leave. I want no more of your crude questions."

The detective turned for the door. As he grabbed the door handle, Mrs. Reed called to him, "Wait! I have a question. Will there be a funeral? Can Emilie have a proper burial?" Mrs. Reed had to ask. She didn't want to hear about one from Connor or that new wife of his. She hoped she never needed to talk with either of them again, but she did want a nice burial for her Emilie.

"I guess that is up to you and Senator Cohen, Ma'am. Good day. Nice talking with you."

"No, it wasn't, Sir, and you know it. Now please, don't come back. Have you no respect for the dead? I want no more ridiculous questions about my daughter's private life. Let her personal life be."

CHAPTER EIGHTEEN

DIG DEEPER

Stanley made such loud charges about Emilie's death, the DA could no longer ignore him. Stanley threatened to arrange a press conference in front of the DA's office and display an over-sized picture he took of the word help on the wall of the boat. He stood prepared to admit to his affair with Emilie and her pregnancy.

Stanley shared his story with a reporter friend who worked for the Democrat Gazette and was prepared to phone reporters in Memphis, Dallas, St. Louis, and Oklahoma City. If necessary, he would contact Chris Matthews or Shawn Hannity. Someone was going to listen to him. The woman he loved and their baby were dead. The public was going to know that Emilie was murdered by her former husband. When he finished, Connor Cohen would be ruined, and if the DA ignored him, he promised to destroy the DA too.

Connor and Abby woke to find a large hand-painted sign posted across the front of their yard that read, 'A murderer lives here.' The reporter from the Democrat Gazette called. He asked if the senator wanted to make a comment since the newspaper had a picture of the sign with Connor's house in the background.

Connor suggested the reporter should talk with his attorney. Stanley was keeping his commitment to ruin Connor.

Connor rushed outside and shredded the sign. Then he phoned Charles, his attorney. The attorney agreed to pursue a restraining order to stop Stanley until the details of Emilie's death could be resolved.

While the reporter posted a subtle hint in the newspaper, he withheld the picture. Connor couldn't blame him. He knew stories about public officials increased readership. Everyone loves gossip, and people hoping to defeat Connor in the next election relished such innuendoes.

As rumors spread, the home phone rang continuously with requests to speak with Connor. Abby and Connor no longer answered it, and Mrs. Vernon was to reply that Connor was unavailable. She should answer no questions about him or Abby or Emilie.

Charles suggested they should hire a private detective to determine who else Emilie might have been seeing. If Stanley wasn't her only lover, this might calm his anger. They definitely needed to find out if Emilie had seen a doctor recently. Was it possible that she was pregnant? He reminded Connor that not all pregnancies are planned.

It took several days to locate the physician who treated Emilie. The PI's assistant, a woman, phoned almost every gynecologist in town. She told each receptionist, "My friend Emilie insists that I should see her doctor. I want to ensure I am calling the correct one." No one saw a woman named Emilie Cohen. However, one did slip and admit they recently saw an Emilie but her name wasn't Cohen. The assistant quickly replied, "Oh, I'm sorry. I forgot. She uses her maiden name, Reed. Is that your Emilie? Sorry. I forgot. Yes, that is her."

The private detective and Charles visited the doctor, but as expected, he refused to discuss Emilie's case. The attorney needed more persuasive power.

Charles met privately with the DA and admitted how they located Emilie's gynecologist. He suggested if they went together to question the doctor, he might be more inclined to talk.

When the physician hesitated, the DA explained bluntly, "It can't be confidential, Doc. She's dead. Dead people no longer have active records. We can get a court order, but if we do that, we promise to disrupt your entire week and dig through all your records. Your office will be swamped with policemen. You won't treat any patients that week. So, make it easy on yourself and on us." The DA used a strong tactic for getting his way.

The physician knew the DA was right. Relenting he admitted, "Yes, Emilie was pregnant, but she didn't realize it at first. She experienced irregular monthly periods for quite a while, as some women do. She definitely did not want the child, but by the time she saw me, it was too late for an abortion."

The doctor paused, and cleared his throat as if he needed to think about what he should say next. "Mrs. Reed, I mean, Mrs. Cohen had another and more serious problem than an unwanted pregnancy. She had syphilis and became angry, even hostile, when I told her. It may be why she gained so little weight. I explained that the effects of syphilis would likely be passed to her baby. After hearing that these babies tend to develop problems in multiple organs, like the brain, eyes, heart, and bones, Mrs. Cohen became hysterical. Thinking she would conceive a child who suffered multiple problems proved more than she could handle.

She demanded that I do an abortion. She pleaded, bribed, and even threatened to ruin me as a doctor. But I don't conduct abortions. For me, abortions are morally wrong. I studied to save lives, not kill them. Besides, she was too far along for anyone to legally perform one. That's when she said that she would go to Asia to have the procedure. I told her she would likely die without proper care, but she insisted she didn't care. She seemed adamant that she preferred death to facing this." The doctor appeared relieved to tell them.

"Since you are required by law to contact all the men she shared sex with, how many names did you get? Did she tell you the name of the man who may have given her syphilis?" The DA continued his questioning, as the attorney watched.

"Well, I thought she did," explained the doctor. "She insisted that she got it from her husband, and said she didn't know what woman he was seeing. At first she told me that I should have my office contact him. Then she changed her mind and made an appointment for her husband to come see me. She said once she told him that he would want to seek medical attention. Only he never came, and when my office phoned the number she gave us, it was a nonworking number. We could find no Hank Reed in the phone book. That's the name she gave us. We tried. You can ask my receptionist."

"We believe you, Doc," said Charles. "But her husband didn't give her syphilis. The two of them had not shared a sexual relationship in years. She was seeing other men, and we may never know who all of them were. However, we do know one, and I will gladly inform him that he needs medical treatment right away. In fact, I will enjoy giving him such news. Thanks for your help."

As they left the doctor's office, the DA said, "Well, that closes this issue. I will mark this case permanently closed. For the family's sake, I think we should leave well enough alone and let our official record remain an accidental death by fire. Nothing could be gained by calling it a suicide. Besides, we have no way of knowing if it was."

The DA promised to take care of the legal details and insisted it might be best if he informed Stanley. "Stanley will come nearer believing it if he hears it from me. I'm not sure he trusts what you might say. Besides, you would enjoy telling him. No one should have that much fun over something this serious. I'll tell him. You inform Connor."

CHAPTER NINETEEN

NEW BEGINNINGS

When Charles arrived at Connor's house, he and Abby were not home. He left word with Mrs. Vernon for Connor to phone him immediately. He wouldn't call and interrupt them. They were at the hospital. Mrs. Reed suffered a heart attack, and her condition appeared serious. She would live, but require permanent, full-time nursing assistance.

Connor and Abby made arrangements to place her at Fox Ridge Nursing Home. She had more than enough money to live the rest of her days in their care. Her daughter from Florida agreed to fly in and complete the billing arrangements. She also offered to take care of having Emilie's remains cremated. She would store them in a nice container and place them in her mother's room.

At long last, Connor felt free of all obligations to the Reed family. Abby, too, liked knowing that Mrs. Reed now lived elsewhere, and she would receive better care than a caretaker provided.

On the drive home, Connor suggested they sell the big house and find another together. He wanted to cut all ties to his past with Emilie.

"But what about the changes I am making in the nursery? I love what's been done so far." Abby admitted.

"Then we can keep the house if you want, but you could find another and remodel all the rooms the way you want them. You could make it all yours. Or we could build if you wanted."

Abby thought for a few minutes. "Could it be smaller? Must we have one so large?"

"You have final say," promised Connor.

"Then, yes. I would like that, but I don't want to build. I think my next year will be too busy." Abby paused. "Well, I do have one condition, and that's if Mrs. Vernon moves with us. Do you think she would agree? She and I have become good friends. I guess she has become my surrogate mother."

"If you and Mrs. Vernon want it to happen, then it will," Connor said smiling. "She has no other family and neither do we. We're a good combination. Like three orphans merging to create a home together."

"Thanks, Connor, but actually there will be four of us. You see, I need her more than ever now because I think I am pregnant. I find out for sure tomorrow when I see the doctor. I didn't want to tell while you worried about Emilie's death."

"Yes! Oh, yes. Abby. That's wonderful. I want to go with you to see the doctor. Oh, I hope you are. I prayed for this since the day we married. It's perfect timing too. I speak at the Stephen's huge fundraising event at the Rockefeller's ranch in three weeks. I will tell everyone that I have no interest in the governorship. In fact, I will announce that I have no plans to seek reelection for senator either."

"But, why?" asked Abby. "You enjoy your work."

"With your good news, as of this moment, my priorities officially change for the better. I want to be a full-time husband, father, and business owner. Nothing else matters. We now have a child to raise."

Dr. Wyveta Kirk is a Christian psychologist, specializing in families and relationships. Her focus is on helping individuals live fuller lives and couples develop closer connections. She spent hours counseling, consulting, coaching, and conducting seminars. She taught for three universities. Dr. Kirk is published in a variety of magazines and professional journals. She speaks frequently on topics of relationship and family concerns.

To inquire about Dr. Kirk's availability for conducting a program, contact her at www.wyvetakirk.com

Dr. Kirk can design a program to fit your needs or you can use one of her tailor-made seminars: Women Talk, Men Walk; -- Help Your Child Feel Loved & Remain Faithful to the Lord; -- Manage Anger; -- and Motivate Others and Yourself.

In addition to her Christian nonfiction novella, Little Rock Secret, she authored:
Women Talk Men Walk: Have the Marriage You Crave, God Tells How, Hormones Explain Why;
Up It's The Only Way to Go; and
Life Cycle and Career Stages of High Achieving Women.